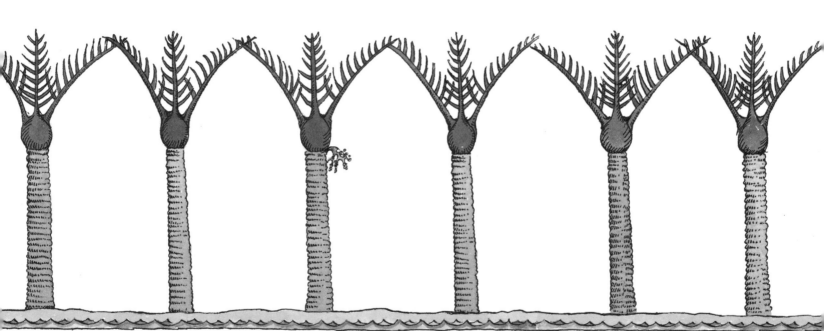

Mr McGee
and the
Big Bag of Bread

Viking

Penguin Group (Australia)
250 Camberwell Road, Camberwell, Victoria 3124, Australia
Penguin Books Ltd
80 Strand, London WC2R 0RL, England
Penguin Group (USA) Inc.
375 Hudson Street, New York, New York 10014, USA
Penguin Books, a division of Pearson Canada
10 Alcorn Avenue, Toronto, Ontario, Canada M4V 3B2
Penguin Group (NZ)
Cnr Airborne and Rosedale Roads, Albany, Auckland 1310, New Zealand
Penguin Books (South Africa) (Pty) Ltd
24 Sturdee Avenue, Rosebank, Johannesburg 2196, South Africa
Penguin Books India (P) Ltd
11, Community Centre, Panchsheel Park, New Delhi 110 017, India

First published by Penguin Group (Australia), a division of
Pearson Australia Group Pty Ltd, 2004

10 9 8 7 6 5 4 3 2 1

Designed by Deborah Brash © Penguin Group (Australia)
Typeset in 26/34pt Berling
Printed and bound by Imago Productions, China

National Library of Australia
Cataloguing-in-Publication data:

Allen, Pamela.
Mr McGee and the big bag of bread.

ISBN 0 670 04239 0.

1. Bread - Juvenile fiction. 2. Zoo animals - Juvenile
fiction. I. Title.

A823.3

www.puffin.com.au

Mr McGee and the Big Bag of Bread was developed from an earlier
title by Pamela Allen, Simon Did, which was first published in 1988
as a small book and has been out of print since 1993.

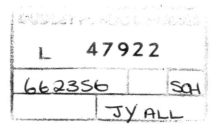

Mr McGee

and the

Big Bag of Bread

Pamela Allen

PENGUIN | VIKING

For Jacob, Ashley, Thomas, Lily, Jayden,
Nikolai, Stefan, Serena, Thomas and Toby

Mr McGee stretched out in his bed.
He gave a big yawn and then he said,
'I don't know what to do today.
Shall I stay in bed, or go out to play?'

'I know what I'll do,' he said.

'I'll visit the animals at the zoo.
I'll pack some bread, to take along, too.'

Do not feed the animals
the notice board said.

But Mr McGee had a big bag of bread.

'Eeeeeee!' howled Mr McGee,

as something hit him, suddenly.

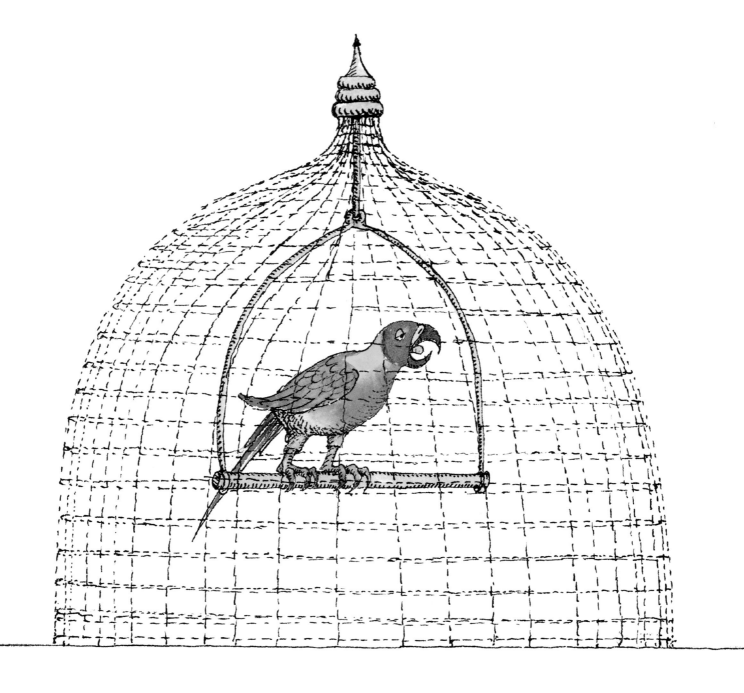

Do not feed the animals
the notice board said.

But Mr McGee had a big bag of bread.

'Eeeeeee!' howled Mr McGee,

as he tried to pull his finger free.

Do not feed the animals
the notice board said.

But Mr McGee had a big bag of bread.

'Eeeeeee!' howled Mr McGee,

as he was hoisted up a tree.

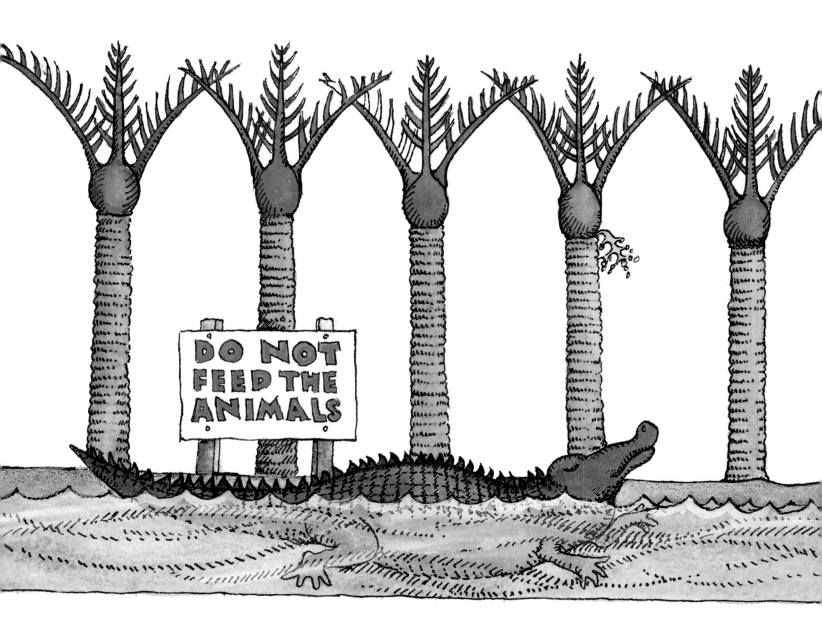

Do not feed the animals
the notice board said.

But Mr McGee had a big bag of bread.

'Eeeeeee!' howled Mr McGee,

as into the water . . .

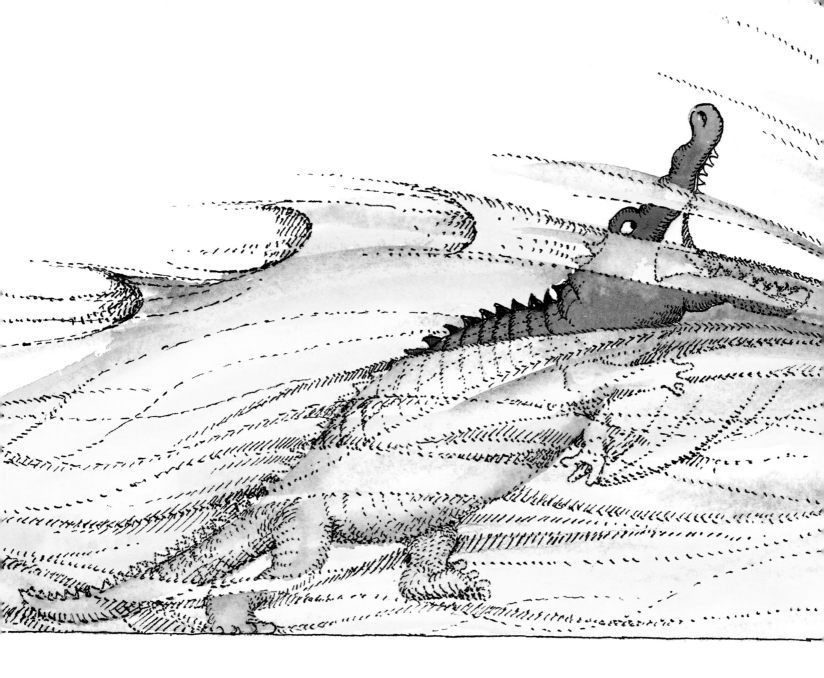

SPLASH! slid he.

Now Mr McGee had lost all his bread.
And *this* crocodile had not been fed!

'EEEEEOOOO

WWWW!' howled Mr McGee.

And up he scrambled into his tree.

The crocodile glared at him, hungrily.

'There's nothing to eat down here,' it said.

So it gobbled up the bed, instead.

Now poor Mr McGee sleeps up in his tree
and tries to keep warm with his cat on his knee.

Do not feed the animals, the notice board said.
Oh, how he wishes he'd stayed in his bed.

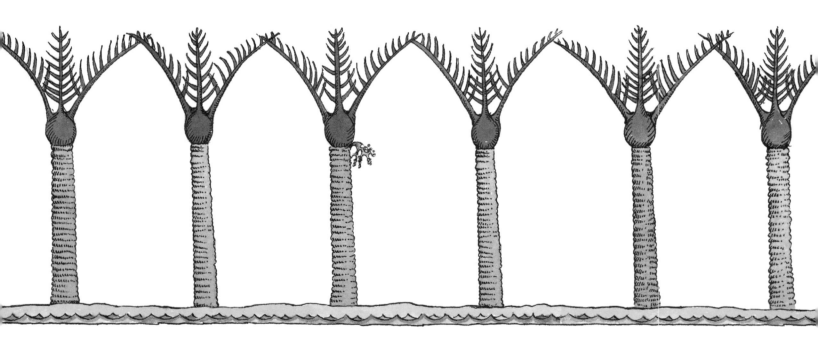